How to Be

by LISA BROWN

HARPERCOLLINSPUBLISHERS

to Otto

Library of Congress Cataloging-in-Publication Data
Brown, Lisa
How to be / by Lisa Brown. — 1st ed.
p.   cm.
Summary: When two children pretend to be various animals, they discover how to be themselves.
ISBN-10: 0-06-054635-2 (trade bdg.) — ISBN-13: 978-0-06-054635-9 (trade bdg.)
ISBN-10: 0-06-054636-0 (lib. bdg.) — ISBN-13: 978-0-06-054636-6 (lib. bdg.)
[1. Animals—Fiction. 2. Self-perception—Fiction.] I. Title.
PZ7.B816145How 2006   2005015147
[E]—dc22

Book design by Alison Donalty
1   3   5   7   9   10   8   6   4   2
❖
First Edition

How to be a
BEAR

Catch fish with your hands.

Hibernate.

Growl.

Be brave.

How to be a
MONKEY

Swing from a tree.

Eat with your toes.

Copy someone.

Be curious.

How to be a
TURTLE

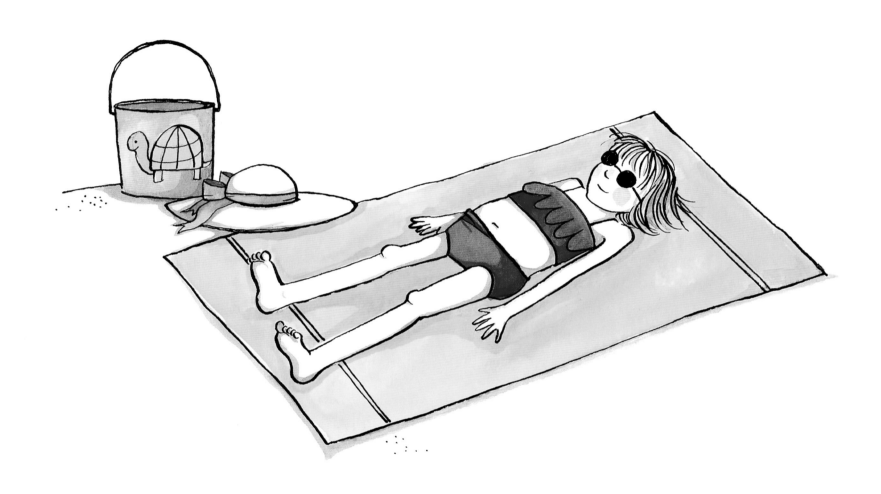

Bask in the sun.

Hide.

Move verrrrrrrry slowly.

Be patient.

How to be a
SNAKE

Shed your skin.

Slither.

Dance in a basket.

Be charming.

How to be a
SPIDER

Creep along walls.

Wait for a meal to come to you.

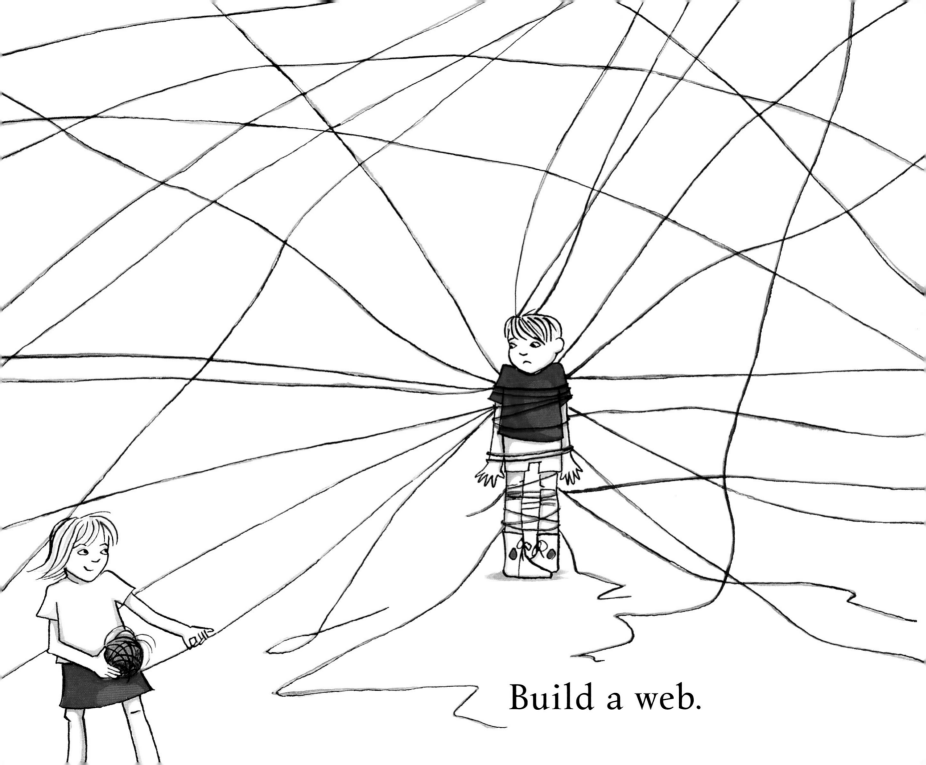

Build a web.

Be creative.

How to be a
DOG

Fetch.

Beg for food.

Lick someone.

Be friendly.

How to be a
PERSON

Be brave, curious,

patient,

charming,

creative, and friendly.....

Be yourself.